Ɖ𝒾𝑠𝓃𝑒𝓎

Family Story Collection

~∞~

Just Be Yourself

Stories About Helping Others and Being Yourself

~∞~

Book Three

Including Characters from Your Favorite Ɖ𝒾𝑠𝓃𝑒𝓎 · **PIXAR** films

Book Three

—⬿⬿⬿—

Just Be Yourself

—⬿⬿⬿—

STORIES ABOUT HELPING OTHERS AND BEING YOURSELF

Introduction

Who am I? How do I fit in? These are questions many children ask themselves. And they are questions that often follow us throughout our lives. Learning to be open to new experiences while being true to ourselves allows us to grow, learn, and discover who we are and who we want to become. Sometimes we find our special place in the world where we least expect it.

In "Lost and Found," Stitch doesn't fit in with the world into which he was born. It's only after he journeys across the galaxy that he figures out where he belongs. For him, home isn't a house or a room or a building, but a little girl, Lilo, with whom he can be himself. In "Go for It!" Flik realizes that he's not the same as those around him. But he discovers that as different as he may be, he has a lot to offer his colony . . . as long as he believes in himself.

Lost and Found

from *Lilo & Stitch*

⚬⚬⚬

Home is a feeling, not just a place.

Stitch was the only one of his kind. A scientist named Jumba had created him in a galaxy far, far away. The Galactic Council wanted to banish Stitch because he was dangerous. "He is the

flawed product of a deranged mind," the council members said. "He has no place among us."

Hearing that he was going to be sent away, Stitch decided to escape.

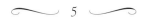

Elsewhere, on a planet called Earth, a little girl named Lilo was feeling very lonely.

One night, Lilo saw a shooting star. She knelt down and wished for a friend who would understand her.

Meanwhile, Stitch had escaped from the Galactic Council. He stole a spaceship and crash-landed on Earth. Someone found him and thought he was a dog, so he wound up in an animal shelter. The next day, Lilo and her sister, Nani, came into the shelter. They adopted Stitch.

Lilo brought Stitch to her house and showed him around. "This is my room," she said. "And this is your bed," she added, pointing to a cardboard box. But Stitch liked Lilo's bed better, so he crawled up on it and grabbed her pillow. Then Stitch looked around. Could this really be his new home?

Later that night, Stitch found a book in Lilo's room. He opened it and saw a picture of a small duck standing alone.

The caption read, "I'm Lost!"

"That's the Ugly Duckling," Lilo explained. "He's sad because he's all alone and nobody wants him. But on this page, his family hears him crying, and they find him. Then the Ugly Duckling is happy because he finds out where he belongs."

Stitch thought about that. The Ugly Duckling had found where he belonged. Could he do the same thing?

For the next few days, Stitch tried hard to fit in. But he kept causing more and more problems in his new home. Maybe he didn't belong there, either.

"If you want to leave, you can," Lilo told him sadly. "I'll remember you. I remember everyone who leaves."

Stitch took the book, *The Ugly Duckling*, and climbed out the window. He walked into the forest. He found a quiet, moonlit spot and looked up at the stars, then down at the book. "Los . . . los . . . lost," he said. "I'M LOST!"

The next morning, the members of the Galactic Council found Stitch in the forest. They wanted to lock him up, far away from everyone. "Don't make me shoot you!" Jumba warned. "Now, come quietly."

Stitch shook his head. "Waiting," he said. He'd finally figured out where he belonged—with Lilo. Even though he hadn't come from Earth, she had helped him feel at home there. And even though he sometimes caused trouble, she was sad when he tried to leave. Now that Stitch had found his true home, he never wanted to leave again.

Go for It!

from *A Bug's Life*

⊗⊗⊗

When you believe in yourself, the sky's the limit.

F lik had been called before Princess Atta and her advisers. "Flik, what do you have to say for yourself?" the Princess demanded.

Flik had accidentally destroyed the food offering that the ants were forced to harvest

for Hopper and his mean gang of
grasshoppers. Now the grasshoppers
demanded twice the amount of food—in
just a few short weeks!

Flik hung his head. "Sorry," he mumbled.
"I didn't mean for things to go so wrong."
Flik always meant well and tried to do his
best. But things
didn't always go
exactly the way
he planned.

While Atta
and the others
discussed Flik's
punishment,
Flik had an idea.
It was perfect.

This idea would take care of those nasty grasshoppers for good!

"We could send someone to get help!" Flik exclaimed.

Atta was shocked. "You mean, leave the island?" she asked. No ant had ever left Ant

Island before.

"There are snakes and birds and bigger bugs out there!" Thorny, one of Atta's advisers, pointed out.

"Exactly!" Flik replied. "We could find bigger bugs to fight for us . . . and forever rid ourselves of Hopper and his gang!"

All the other ants thought Flik was crazy. Besides, which ant would be brave enough to leave the island?

It wasn't until Flik volunteered to go that Princess Atta and her advisers changed their tune.

Dr. Flora whispered to Atta, "You see, with Flik gone . . ."

". . . he can't mess anything up!" Atta whispered back. The decision was made.

As Flik set off, some of the ants gathered to watch him go. No one believed Flik would make it.

No one except Princess Dot. She liked Flik. She had faith that he would bring back the meanest, toughest bugs to battle Hopper. "He knows what he's doing," she said.

"That's right!" Flik said as he shinned up a dandelion stalk. At the top, he tore one wispy seed sack from the flower. "Here we go!" Flik shouted. "For the colony, and for oppressed ants everywhere!"

With that, he jumped off the flower, still clinging to the dandelion seed. It

caught on a breeze and carried Flik through the air and across the ravine. So what if Dot was the only ant who had faith in him? Flik believed in himself and he knew that he could save the colony. And that's what kept him going as he set off into the big, wide world.